I0741564

Mercury

by Steve Yockey

MUSIC AND THIRD-PARTY MATERIALS USE NOTE

IMPORTANT BILLING AND CREDIT REQUIREMENTS

MERCURY premiered at Salt Lake Acting Company (Cynthia Fleming, Executive Artistic Director) on October 11, 2017. The production was directed by Shannon Musgrave, with scenic design by Gage Williams, costumes by Philip R. Lowe, lighting by James M. Craig, sound by Cynthia L. Kehr Rees, prop design by Janice Jenson, projection design by Michael Horejsi, and puppet design and construction by Linda L. Brown & Steven Glenn Brown. The Production Stage Manager was Justin Ivie. The cast was as follows:

PAMELA .... Dee-Dee Darby-Duffin
HEATHER .... Brighton Hertford
ALICIA....................................... Lily Hye Soo Dixon
OLIVE... April Fossen
NICK ....Max Cedar Huftalin
BRIAN ....Tito Livas
SAM... Aaron Adams

CHARACTERS

PAMELA – a married woman, definitely type A, used to getting her way in most things, and probably pretty lonely

HEATHER – a married woman, charismatic and poised, used to relying on a friendly smile to smooth things over

ALICIA – a woman, chatty with a "new age" vibe, she vacillates between flighty and ominous, steeped in the occult

OLIVE – a woman, a downstairs neighbor, someone who thinks of herself as good and correct, myopic, also a busybody

NICK – a man, a solid communicator, he's doing an okay job of holding it together, staying positive; the strong one

BRIAN – a man, handsome and flippant, definitely an urbanite, still learning how to really commit during hard times

SAM – Alicia's boyfriend; he's not an angry guy, just very matter of fact, easily frustrated, and usually bloody; he's also the physical manifestation of vengeance

SETTING

In and around Portland, OR.

AUTHOR'S NOTES

[ ] indicate overlapping dialogue.

The set is essentially a wooden platform with everything needed during the play. The platform is on a "revolve" with one of four locales set on each side. No walls. Everything can be seen. Alicia is the only force visibly turning the stage between scenes, accompanied by large mechanical sounds. It looks like hard work. Behind the set, an immense scrim or screen looms. It is only used during Scene Six. **This description is meant to be a useful place to start exploring how this play lives onstage**.

For a short time, a moon of Mercury was thought to exist. On March 27, 1974, two days before the Mariner 10 probe made its flyby of the planet, instruments began registering large amounts of ultraviolet radiation in the vicinity that, according to one astronomer, "had no right to be there." But by the next day, the radiation had disappeared. It then reappeared three days later, seeming to originate from an object independent of Mercury. Shortly thereafter, this flickering "moon" was explained away simply as a star making noise in the background of the sensors.

One

(A kitchen. **PAMELA** *is seated at a table. Jeans and a T-shirt. Another chair sits empty. A variety of small cacti are arranged in front of her on the table. Maybe there are a half dozen, maybe even more. There is also a small spray bottle and a glass tumbler. It's a very generous scotch on the rocks.)*

(She is quietly humming a little tune to herself and rearranging the order of the cacti. The doorbell rings. She ignores it. There is a knock. She ignores that, too.)

(**HEATHER** *tiptoes in wearing an easy dress with a cardigan. She stops short. She clearly didn't know anyone was home. For her part,* **PAMELA** *is distracted, but almost aggressively bright and chipper.)*

HEATHER. Oh! Oh, hi. You're here. I didn't know you were home.

PAMELA. I suppose that's why you used your key?

HEATHER. I did knock first. And rang the doorbell, [but you...?]

PAMELA. [Mmhm, I] heard you, I was busy. I am arranging my new cacti into a pleasing configuration before I decide where to place them. I'm getting a feel for them.

HEATHER. All right?

PAMELA. Trial and error. Oh, did you need some sugar? Did you need to borrow a cup of sugar? That's what a neighbor does, right? We're being neighborly so I assume you came to borrow a cup of sugar, or take a cup of sugar as it were.

HEATHER. You know I don't bake.

PAMELA. Yes, I do know that. Then did you need some fabric softener?

HEATHER. You don't have to do all this, Pamela.

PAMELA. What do you need, Heather? I don't know what you imagine, but these cacti will not arrange themselves and I have other things to do before my husband gets home.

HEATHER. Like finish your scotch?

PAMELA. Like finish my scotch, yes.

> *(She finishes the entire tumbler of scotch in one swig.)*

HEATHER. Okay, I can tell you're not in the mood to chat right now.

PAMELA. Can you?

HEATHER. I came over looking for Mr. Bundles, have you seen him?

PAMELA. Why would your dog be inside my house?

HEATHER. He's been missing since last night and I know you keep those treats for him so I thought maybe he… snuck in and you didn't realize?

PAMELA. You thought perhaps your Cavalier King Charles Spaniel "snuck" into my house for treats and I somehow didn't notice?

HEATHER. He is a smart dog. But when you say it like that it doesn't sound very plausible.

PAMELA. We have motion sensors.

HEATHER. All right.

PAMELA. We have motion sensors that beep and send messages directly to our phones.

HEATHER. I get it.

> (**PAMELA** *chuckles to herself.*)

PAMELA. You don't need to manufacture a reason to come over.

HEATHER. Mr. Bundles is missing.

PAMELA. If you say so.

> (*She pours herself more scotch.*)

Do you want some?

HEATHER. I shouldn't. Jimmy will be home soon. If he smells it on me, he starts spinning out into these silly guilt fantasies that I'm drinking away ennui. He's so hard on himself.

PAMELA. Perfect.

> (*She toasts and then drinks the scotch again.
> The whole glass.*)

HEATHER. Oh my.

PAMELA. You should ask how I've been, shouldn't you?

> (*Pause.*)

Since yesterday? How have I been since yesterday when you left me in a heap on the floor of my living room with the vacuum cleaner running like soul crushing white noise? I've been fine.

HEATHER. You turned on the vacuum cleaner to try to avoid me; you did that.

PAMELA. Aren't you perceptive?

HEATHER. Look, it took me hours to work up the nerve to talk to you. I wasn't going to let some light housework stop me.

PAMELA. Clearly.

HEATHER. So it's your fault that I had to yell and it's my fault I ran away so we both could have handled it better and I didn't come over here to rehash any of this, I'm just looking for Mr. Bundles. If you're hiding him, it's not funny. And he needs his eye drops.

PAMELA. Are you fucking serious?

HEATHER. Honey, he needs eye drops every morning. He's predisposed to glaucoma.

PAMELA. You're a saint.

HEATHER. It can't be a coincidence that he's missing now.

PAMELA. Do you like these cacti? I've never been a fan, you know me: perennials, perennials. And sure, maybe some ornamental grasses. But I was at the home goods store this morning and there they were, like a field of little anti-social tombstones in a dim corner. I just started putting them in my basket one [after another.]

HEATHER. [Pamela, I] meant I do not believe it's a coincidence he's missing.

PAMELA. I'm sorry your dog is missing, but I have no clues to help you and my spiny friends here require my attention. Actually, they require very little attention, or water, they're succulents. They're fleshy. They practically take care of themselves.

> (*She picks up the spray bottle and sprays a bit.*)

In fact, I don't even need this. I don't even know why [I bought it.]

HEATHER. [Jesus, enough] about the cacti.

PAMELA. They're literally designed so you can't touch them, isn't that [fascinating?]

HEATHER. [I don't want to] talk about the cacti.

PAMELA. And I don't want to talk at all, so that works perfectly!

(Pause.)

HEATHER. Look, it wasn't easy, emotionally or because of the fucking vacuum, to tell you that we shouldn't do what we were doing [anymore and...]

*(**PAMELA** starts laughing.)*

PAMELA. ["Do what we] were doing?"

HEATHER. Yes, do what [we were doing.]

PAMELA. [Have sex! Have] sex. For the love of God, just say "have sex," we were having regular, secretive, really [satisfying sex.]

HEATHER. [Shhhh. Keep] your voice down.

PAMELA. You don't need to be bashful and talk around it, there's no one [else here!]

HEATHER. [I'm not] interested in broadcasting our very [private business.]

PAMELA. [You're unbelievable,] I am in disbelief! Who do you think is going to hear me? We were having sex! We were having sex and enjoying a connection. And being a little less lonely, or I thought that's what we were doing. That's what I was doing.

HEATHER. We were also sneaking around, sneaking around wracked with guilt over a little bit of pleasure and I am not that lonely. I am not. You can be a cliché if you want to be a cliché, but I will no longer [indulge...]

PAMELA. [A cliché?!]

HEATHER. Yes! And I won't indulge that.

PAMELA. Well, this smacks of a prepared speech.

HEATHER. And the very same night our dog is missing.

PAMELA. And you're accusing me of what exactly?

HEATHER. I'm not accusing. I'm investigating.

PAMELA. Okay, I see. Now you think I'm some other cliché, right? That I sloughed off the "lonely housewife" routine for a little bit to try out "scorned lover."

> *(She sprays at **HEATHER** with the spray bottle. **HEATHER** backs away.)*

HEATHER. Stop it.

> *(She sprays again, **HEATHER** moves around the table to avoid her.)*

PAMELA. Am I a psychopath, is that what you [think?]

HEATHER. [No!]

> *(She chases **HEATHER** around the table, spraying her.)*

PAMELA. Am I criminally psychotic, Heather? Am I crazed [and vengeful?!]

HEATHER. [No, of course] not! Pamela, stop it!

> *(**PAMELA** stops and sets down the spray bottle.)*

PAMELA. No, I'm just your neighbor and things got complicated and things got hurtful. For me, I was hurt. But why on Earth would I do anything to your dog? [Why would...?]

HEATHER. [It hurts me,] too!

PAMELA. Does it?

HEATHER. I'm not heartless; of course it hurts. But it was never going to be anything more. I'm sorry, honey, but that was never going to happen. This was, maybe I shouldn't have come over [here today.]

PAMELA. [Maybe, but you] did! And you will, you'll come over for your dog, or some sugar, or some dryer sheets, or some heavy cream or cotton balls or whatever. It's not like we can avoid each other; you live next door. Right next door, a butterfly bush, a tiny little garden wall, then nothing but the sunlight through the kitchen window of your meticulously-restored Craftsman home and then you.

HEATHER. Honey, I'm sure after some time has passed, [we can...]

PAMELA. [Yep!]

(*Pause.* **PAMELA** *sits back down and begins to fiddle with the cacti.* **HEATHER** *sits down, taps the table nervously, and then gets up, launching into her speech...*)

HEATHER. I never meant to hurt you.

(**PAMELA** *mimes shooting herself.*)

I never meant to hurt you and you know that. Yes, I was swept up in the romance of, in the illicit way we were together. And I want to apologize for getting carried away, or if I made you think that it could be more.

PAMELA. Which you did.

HEATHER. So I do want to apologize and I would have apologized yesterday if you had just turned off the goddamned vacuum cleaner. You're so beautiful, Pamela. And so unexpected. And just very, very special to me. And I love that you're right next door. I love...that. But I can't lie to Jimmy anymore and, really, I don't want to.

PAMELA. I don't want to lie to Mike, either. It doesn't feel good.

HEATHER. You see?

> (**PAMELA** *begins to break, but she fights it. Focused on her cacti, she will not fully cry in front of* **HEATHER** *if she can help it.*)

PAMELA. But this doesn't feel good either.

HEATHER. I know.

PAMELA. This doesn't feel good.

HEATHER. I know.

PAMELA. And I guess I am lonely. Clichés are clichés for a reason.

HEATHER. Honey, I know.

PAMELA. I'm just... No, I'm fine. It's fine.

> (*Pause.*)

HEATHER. I'm sorry I snuck into your house; I really don't know what I was thinking.

PAMELA. You were looking for Mr. Bundles.

HEATHER. Maybe that was a convenient excuse. Well not convenient, but he hasn't been gone that long. I'm sure I'm just being silly.

PAMELA. That can happen. You're silly and I'm just...

> (*She exhales releasing all of the tension from her body.*)

HEATHER. Okay. Okay.

PAMELA. I should get back to this.

HEATHER. Honey, I don't understand what you're doing with the cacti.

PAMELA. I know.

HEATHER. All right. Well, we'll... I know! We'll have you and Mike over for dinner next week. How about that?

> *(This is pretty clearly the worst idea* **PAMELA** *has ever heard.)*

A nice dinner with all four of us, yes. And things will start to feel normal. We'll make them normal, okay? We will make them normal.

PAMELA. Okay.

HEATHER. There's nothing we can't make right.

PAMELA. Nothing?

HEATHER. Not a thing.

> *(***PAMELA*** *pours another scotch.)*

Now I need to find Mr. Bundles. Poor little guy, who knows where he'll end up?

PAMELA. Of course.

HEATHER. Sometimes I think that dog is too clever for his own good.

PAMELA. Heather, you should look...

> *(Pause.)*

I know you don't like gardening. But you should take some gloves and one of my trowels and dig behind that butterfly bush you gave me last spring. Where the dirt is freshly overturned. You won't have to dig very deep.

> *(***HEATHER*** *stares in disbelief.* **PAMELA** *might even relish this moment.)*

HEATHER. Pamela.

PAMELA. There's nothing we can't make right.

> *(She drinks her scotch. **HEATHER** covers her mouth and rushes out.)*

Two

(A store. **OLIVE** *is waiting at a counter. She's shopping for something very specific. This store only sells very specific things. She's wearing an odd hat of some kind. Not a fascinator or anything, maybe just an old sun hat.)*

*(***ALICIA*** *enters from the back in overalls and a tank top. Her hair is pulled back in a ponytail. She's polishing a large serrated knife. She has on gloves. She stops when she sees* **OLIVE**, *smiles, and takes her place behind the counter.)*

(There is a desk bell on the counter. It sits in front of a device that could be a vintage dictaphone or some early radio-like machine. It's really something else all together.)

ALICIA. Nice to see you, Olive, sorry about the wait. I just had to move something; Sam always leaves me with these little odd jobs, so annoying. Have you been here long?

OLIVE. Not at all.

ALICIA. You can always just ring the little bell.

(She rings the little bell with the blade of the knife.)

OLIVE. You know, I just don't like to be a bother and the sound is so jarring.

ALICIA. Well, it is a bell. But aren't you considerate?

OLIVE. I suppose I am.

ALICIA. You know I was actually telling Sam, my boyfriend Sam, I was telling him last night that he could be, like, more considerate, should be more considerate, I mean just because he provides all of the odds and ends for my shop that doesn't mean he gets to boss me around or set the hours or any of those other like assertive male maneuvers, ya know? It's my shop. Mine. And he needs to respect [that truth.]

OLIVE. [Of course.]

ALICIA. I mean it's so insidious, these little, these little microaggressions, like these little tiny dominations, and I just won't stand for it, not [at all.]

OLIVE. [That's right.]

ALICIA. Not from a man who is supposed to be in love with me. I mean we've been together for I don't even want to tell you how long now and look, no ring. Well, like, you can't see because of the glove, but trust me there's no ring. No promises, ya know? And even if he did up and propose all of the sudden, he still doesn't own me. And I told him, I told Sam, that exact thing.

OLIVE. Good for you. I've always said that people have to stand up for themselves, simple as that. Even when it's hard, even when it feels like you're the only one in the world who understands how to make something right.

ALICIA. Yes. Thank you. Thanks, Olive.

OLIVE. And what did he say?

ALICIA. He was working. I sort of interrupted his work, which is a big "no no." So he said we'd talk about it later and I agreed.

OLIVE. Oh, now I see.

ALICIA. I know how that sounds, but I could tell from his eyes that he, like, really heard me.

OLIVE. I hope you're right, but…it honestly doesn't sound promising.

ALICIA. Well that's not exactly supportive, Olive.

OLIVE. Oh, all right. Then I meant, "I'm sure it will be just fine."

ALICIA. Well now I'm worried about it. Ugh, I just hate it when things feel off. Oh, you know what? I bet Mercury is in retrograde. I can feel it. Is Mercury in retrograde? Is that happening right now?

OLIVE. I don't know what that means.

ALICIA. You don't know about astrology?

OLIVE. No, I've [never really…]

ALICIA. [It's just that] you seem like the type. To me.

OLIVE. What type is that?

ALICIA. Someone who puts her stock in…the greater workings of things.

OLIVE. Well, you've read me wrong there. I pride myself on the practical, keep my feet planted right here on the ground, thank you. I have very little interest in any of that astrology business and I've certainly never given Mercury a second thought. I wouldn't even know where to look for it in the sky.

ALICIA. You can't see it because of the sun and you'd just go blind, pop, pop, nothing.

OLIVE. That's unsettling.

ALICIA. Right? So here's the deal: when Mercury is in retrograde it basically looks like it's moving backwards across the sky. It's not, I mean obviously, because planets only go in one [direction.]

OLIVE. [Yes, yes,] of course.

ALICIA. But it looks that way. And that bright little fucker just cruising along, well, it screws up communication, honesty, your brain, not "your brain," but my brain, just all kinds of things. I think that might be why Sam's been in such a bad mood. And I can't believe it's just now occurring to me, I can be so dense sometimes.

(She bops herself in the side of the head playfully with the hilt of the knife.)

OLIVE. You should be careful with that knife.

ALICIA. No one's going to get stabbed or anything.

*(Suddenly the sound of static comes from the odd dictaphone. It comes in a burst, not loud but surprising. **OLIVE** gasps.)*

*(Buried in the static, a **VOICE** can barely be heard. We can only make out pieces of it rising and falling in waves under the static, if anything. But the full text is here:)*

SAM. Please get down here now or I will drown you in an ocean of blood.

*(**ALICIA** rolls her eyes, picks up the funnel of the dictaphone, and speaks into it.)*

ALICIA. Sorry. I can't understand what you're saying.

(She hangs up the funnel and flips a switch, turning off the machine.)

OLIVE. I'm sorry, but did...did someone say something about an "ocean of blood"?

ALICIA. Olive, don't be crazy. That was just Sam, why would he say that?

OLIVE. That's what it sounded like.

ALICIA. Who can even tell with all the static, but he insists on using these things. Junk. I swear he's just headache after headache. Sometimes I think about leaving him, but I just can't. Ugh, listen to me rattle on like a broken furnace. How can I help you?

> (**OLIVE** *removes her hat and sets it on the counter.* **ALICIA** *eyes the hat like it shouldn't be there.*)

OLIVE. Well, you remember my upstairs neighbor, the older woman who I told you so much about the last time I came in?

ALICIA. Sure, the one who kept taking up both parking places in your duplex?

OLIVE. Among other things, yes, that's her. And after I went out of my way to be a good neighbor, but let me not get riled up again. I prefer not to be angry.

ALICIA. That's healthy.

OLIVE. And the item you sold me last time really helped resolve things.

ALICIA. So great…

> (**ALICIA** *puts down the knife and picks up Olive's hat.*)

This is off topic and I feel awkward about asking, but can I hand this to you?

OLIVE. I'm sorry?

ALICIA. I know, it's just that it's pretty warm outside and I'm sure you've been perspiring and I'd rather not have your hat sitting on the counter. You understand, I know.

OLIVE. Oh. Oh, of course, Alicia.

> (*She takes the hat and holds it.*)

ALICIA. Ugh, that's so great, thanks so much. I was feeling so awkward, it was hard to listen because I could literally feel the sweaty moisture violating my countertop and who needs that distraction? Now, please continue. I promise, I'm totally focused. Really.

OLIVE. I am sorry about the hat, if [I had...]

ALICIA. [Don't give it] another thought.

OLIVE. Okay. Well as I've said, you really helped.

ALICIA. Efficacy means repeat business. You certainly prove that.

> *(They both laugh again. It's dark.)*

OLIVE. But now she's ailing, unfortunately, so her son has come to stay in her unit.

ALICIA. And he's an asshole?

OLIVE. On the contrary, he's very nice. Thoughtful, courteous, and not too bad to look at if you know what I mean.

> *(They share a knowing chuckle.* **ALICIA** *does know.)*

The trouble is that he's brought a friend with him. A close "friend." And that friend is not as nice. Or thoughtful. Or courteous.

ALICIA. But not too bad to look at?

> *(***OLIVE** *doesn't chuckle this time.)*

OLIVE. I can hear them, you see. I can hear everything that happens in that unit above me. And this friend is a bad person. When he's not yelling and whining, he's saying hurtful things to Nick. Or about me, sometimes about me, and I haven't done anything but try to be neighborly and supportive in this time of need. And when Nick is out during the day visiting his mom or taking care of things, sometimes this "friend" has… other friends over. To relax. That's not the right word. And I have to listen as they do filthy things behind Nick's back. Honestly, Alicia, it is ruining my quality of life.

ALICIA. Olive, that's awful.

OLIVE. It is awful, yes. And Nick is such a dear man, in my estimation.

ALICIA. Mmhm.

OLIVE. I really believe he'd be so much better off without all of the extra drama. And certainly the duplex would be quieter.

ALICIA. Mmhm.

OLIVE. And because Nick's "friend" is so awful, I thought you might have something. To help remedy the situation.

ALICIA. Well you're familiar with the stock, is there something you had in [mind to…]

OLIVE. [That's the] thing, if I may, I was hoping for something a little more potent.

ALICIA. Potent?

OLIVE. Immediate?

ALICIA. Oh no, you're angling for our higher-end items and [those aren't…]

OLIVE. [Wonderful, does] "higher-end" mean stronger [or just…?]

ALICIA. [No, Olive,] they aren't for everyday problems.

OLIVE. I think I've made the case that this isn't an "everyday problem."

ALICIA. I don't know.

OLIVE. I sincerely need your help, Alicia. Your expeditious help.

ALICIA. Sam wouldn't like it.

> (**OLIVE** *puts her hand on* **ALICIA***'s gloved hand.*)

OLIVE. Well...it isn't Sam's shop.

> (*Pause.*)

ALICIA. As it happens...I may have something.

OLIVE. Oh, thank goodness.

> (*She carefully brings a small, thin, black book from behind the counter and sets it down.* **OLIVE** *reaches to touch it and* **ALICIA** *slaps her hand.*)

ALICIA. Don't touch it! Never touch it.

OLIVE. Oh.

> (*As* **ALICIA** *speaks, she produces some brown butcher paper and string from behind the counter and carefully wraps the book.*)

ALICIA. You'll want to give this as a gift to Nick's special "friend" and make sure that he's the only one who opens it. Now assuming you're accurate and this friend has been straying and telling lies, generally "doing wrong," then all he'll have to do is touch it.

OLIVE. Then what?

ALICIA. Then problem solved. Now, I cannot stress to you enough that this is one of our higher-end items. That means, as per usual but a bit more than usual, if anything goes awry then there may be additional costs and penalties.

OLIVE. What does that mean?

ALICIA. It means "additional costs and penalties."

OLIVE. No, of course, but what are those specifically?

ALICIA. Don't worry, it'll all be fine. It's always fine, isn't it?

(*She has finished wrapping the book.*)

OLIVE. No complaints thus far.

ALICIA. You see? There you go. Okay, all set. So for you the total today will be $287. That's with the discount. You get a discount for being such a...good customer.

OLIVE. It is my favorite shop in the city.

ALICIA. You know, we actually have locations in a lot of cities now.

OLIVE. Is that right? Well, it wouldn't be the same without you.

ALICIA. You'd be surprised. They're all run by someone exactly like me. It's almost like they're all the same shop.

OLIVE. How...cryptic? Let me just...

(**OLIVE** *sets her hat down on the counter again in order to dig through her purse for her wallet.* **ALICIA** *exhales and picks up the knife again. And forcefully stabs the knife down into the counter.*)

ALICIA. Olive. I really do like you, but if you don't get your sweaty hat off my counter then I'm going to take all of your hair off and any skin that comes along with it.

(**OLIVE** *grabs her hat and clutches it to her chest. She drops some money on the counter.* **ALICIA** *totally relaxes, pulls the knife out of the counter, and sets it down. She picks up the money and begins to count.*)

I'll just get your change and you'll be ready to go.

OLIVE. No, no, that's okay. You keep the change. Really.

ALICIA. That is just so sweet. Sam won't believe me when I tell him; he thinks everyone is just the worst.

> (**OLIVE** *slips the wrapped book off the counter and heads for the door.*)

OLIVE. Oh! Heavier than it looks, isn't it?

ALICIA. It's full of help. You have a great day. And let me know how that book works out for your friend's "friend."

> (**OLIVE** *exits quickly.* **ALICIA** *polishes the knife. Suddenly the sound of static comes from the odd dictaphone. It comes in a burst, not loud, but surprising. Buried in the static, a* **VOICE** *can barely be heard again. And the voice is yelling...*)

SAM. Alicia! I know you can hear me. Alicia!

> (**ALICIA** *rolls her eyes, reaches over, and shuts it off.*)

Three

(A living room. **BRIAN** *is in his underwear and a T-shirt sitting in a chair.* **NICK** *is perched on the edge of the table in pajama pants with his head in his hands. He's a little bit exasperated but doing his best to keep things positive.)*

NICK. We're not getting a shotgun.

BRIAN. Well I don't think a handgun is going to do it, Nick.

NICK. We're not getting any gun of any kind at all.

BRIAN. "We" don't have to do anything.

NICK. I will not have a gun in this house, Brian.

BRIAN. I'm talking about the car. It was at the car, right there looking [at me.]

NICK. [And nothing] happened.

BRIAN. Because I turned to stone behind the wheel and waited for it to go away, because I sat there like a [statue until...]

NICK. [It was just] digging through the trash.

> *(***NICK*** *walks over and straddles* **BRIAN**, *sitting on his lap facing him. He rests his arms on* **BRIAN***'s shoulders.)*

BRIAN. Oh, the trash you're not supposed to put out until the morning because it might attract bears? Because we fucking live somewhere now that has golden rules about bears?

NICK. I forgot.

> *(***NICK*** *begins to kiss* **BRIAN***'s neck as* **BRIAN** *continues. He's probably getting handsy too but* **BRIAN** *isn't having it.)*

BRIAN. You're not the one who comes home late at night, so why should you worry if bears come and dig through the trash. It's not like you're going to end up in a stare down with one of them at midnight after a twelve-hour shift with absolutely no way to protect yourself.

> (**NICK** *gives up on the kissing and climbs off of* **BRIAN.** *He adjusts himself in his pajama pants and is clearly a little disappointed.*)

NICK. I want to figure out how to acknowledge your point and still let you know that you're making way too big a deal about this.

BRIAN. You're failing.

NICK. I'm sorry that a bear looked at you, okay?

BRIAN. It's so easy to joke, right? What if I hadn't been paying attention?

NICK. I don't think the bear would have attacked you.

BRIAN. Oh, did you know the bear in question?

NICK. And in case you didn't notice, I was trying to make it up to you by offering myself up as penance, because I am magnanimous.

BRIAN. It's bad enough we had to move here, let [alone...]

NICK. [Oh, no.]

BRIAN. Excuse me, but [I'm not...]

NICK. [Absolutely] not. Look, I deeply regret that you were frightened by a wild animal that was probably equally frightened of you and I will sit here and listen to all of your anxiety about that situation and deal with the fact you're too pissed off to fuck, but I will not engage in some worn-out debate about moving again. That debate is over; it's done.

BRIAN. I don't think so.

NICK. Okay, well, we already moved, [so...?]

BRIAN. [I can count] on no hands the number of times I was attacked by a bear [in Portland.]

NICK. [You've never] been attacked by a bear here either!

BRIAN. Last night!

NICK. Go on and show me the bear-related injury [right now.]

BRIAN. [You're not] listening.

NICK. I am. I hear you, Brian. I hear you when you complain about the mountain fog even though it's beautiful. I hear you when you complain that it's too cold even though it's roughly the same temperature as Portland. I hear you when you complain that you might die by crashing into a deer in the road because you fucking drive too fast like you're in a race to get everywhere. I hear you when you complain that your shifts at the hospital are boring now even though you used to come home every night in the city crazed, hating life, and nursing a sprained wrist from some tweaked-out meth head. And I hear you about the scary fucking bears. You are heard.

BRIAN. The meth head thing happened exactly one time.

NICK. I love you. We live here now. Deal with it. I'm making coffee.

> (**NICK** *heads into the kitchen area and begins making coffee.*)

BRIAN. I'm not done talking [about this.]

NICK. [I'm making] coffee.

BRIAN. I'm not happy.

NICK. You'll live.

BRIAN. You're supposed to care that I'm not happy.

NICK. We're here because my mom doesn't have a lot of time left, and this is where we have to be until whenever [that's over.]

BRIAN. [You don't have] to remind [me why we're…]

NICK. [And we have] no idea how long that'll be and thanks for making me say that awful truth out loud. Again. This is something that's [not an option.]

BRIAN. [If I didn't love] you, I wouldn't be fighting about it. I'd just leave.

NICK. Perfect, the leaving thing again. You've started playing this card [a lot, Brian.]

BRIAN. [So I can love] you and still talk about leaving a less-than-ideal situation.

NICK. Fantastic, we love each other!

BRIAN. Don't get loud.

NICK. Oh no! We might attract the bears.

BRIAN. You can go to hell sometimes, you know.

NICK. Bears! Bears!

BRIAN. Ugh, just make the coffee. Some of us have to go back to work this morning.

> (**NICK** *opens and closes his fists, shaking off the anger.*)

NICK. Oh. Okay. Well, "some of us" gave up our jobs and now spend our time here or lost in a creepy storage unit for hours sorting through a lifetime and packing up for some of our mom's looming deaths. Sorry if you feel "put upon."

BRIAN. I'm feeling like coffee would help.

> (*There's a knock at the door. Well, four sharp knocks. If you're familiar with Japanese*

superstitions, you might think death is at the door. If you're not, it's just annoyingly persistent.)

*(**BRIAN** crashes down into a chair and picks up a magazine.)*

NICK. If I'm making the coffee, you can get the door.

BRIAN. I'm not wearing clothes.

NICK. When the fuck did you get bashful?

BRIAN. We both know who it is and I'm not interested.

NICK. She's just being neighborly.

BRIAN. She's at the door all the time. And she's visiting your mom all the time. I see her at the hospital every day. She's always everywhere. And she wants to fuck you.

NICK. That's just in your head and she can probably hear you.

(Four knocks again.)

BRIAN. Well you can talk about it at one of your cute little lunches.

NICK. She's a good listener.

BRIAN. $20 says she opens with, "I heard shouting…"

NICK. Fine.

BRIAN. Shouting. $20.

NICK. I said fine. Stop trying to bet me when I already took the bet.

*(Four knocks again. It's not more intense. It's almost infuriatingly exactly the same every time. **BRIAN** grunts and loudly whispers…)*

BRIAN. Ugh, even her knock drives me crazy.

*(**NICK** opens the door to reveal **OLIVE**. Smiling. A tight smile, but it's unclear if **OLIVE** has an easy smile. She has the wrapped-up book under one arm.)*

NICK. Hi, Olive. How are you?

OLIVE. I'm so sorry to bother you, but I heard yelling?

NICK. Everything's fine.

OLIVE. It was just the yelling, or else I wouldn't have [come up.]

BRIAN. [Hello,] Olive.

OLIVE. Hello.

BRIAN. How's downstairs?

OLIVE. Fine.

BRIAN. Good. I'm sorry I didn't dress up for your visit.

OLIVE. You didn't dress at all.

BRIAN. It is early.

OLIVE. That's maybe why the yelling scared me; the walls are just so thin, Nick, I can't help but overhear things, you know?

BRIAN. It'd be the ceiling wouldn't it? Your ceiling is too thin?

OLIVE. Nick, I want you to know that I specifically said "yelling" instead of "shouting" so Brian would lose the $20 bet I shouldn't have overheard but did anyway because it was so loud.

BRIAN. You overhear a lot.

OLIVE. Hard not to.

NICK. We're not used to having neighbors so we're still calibrating our volume.

BRIAN. You tell her the same thing every time.

NICK. Brian was almost attacked by a bear last night, so he's cranky.

OLIVE. Oh my, was he hurt?

NICK. No.

OLIVE. Oh.

BRIAN. Try not to sound too disappointed.

NICK. The bear looked at him.

BRIAN. No dangerous bears in Portland.

NICK. No dangerous meth addicts here.

OLIVE. Oh, I've read about that, the "meth amphetamine," what an awful drug. Don't you ever just wish people could be nicer to themselves?

BRIAN. You know what? I'm gonna take a shower.

(**BRIAN** *exits into the back of the apartment.*)

NICK. He's really not that bad.

OLIVE. It's none of my business. But you've been so nice since you moved in, I just feel like if I hear something it's my job to check it out. And based on the stories you've told me during our lunches at Soup and Sides, he just seems volatile.

NICK. You shouldn't worry. No one should have to worry about anything at Soup and Sides, except eating too much.

(**OLIVE** *laughs too aggressively and touches* **NICK***'s arm.*)

OLIVE. It is delicious.

NICK. Oh, and Brian mentioned you've been visiting my mom in the hospital?

OLIVE. It's just so sad. I know it must be hard for you, all of this. And I know you can't be there all the time and Brian can only stop in for a few minutes now and then, barely any time at all. But I'm happy to be there with her. Watch her go through this. She was always so very kind to me, you know?

NICK. And you are very kind to her.

OLIVE. It's nothing.

NICK. All right, I should probably finish making the coffee now. Or Brian will be even more of a grump [and I can't...]

OLIVE. [Oh, of course,] but actually I did come up for another reason. It almost seems silly now, but I brought this for Brian, believe it or not. Almost slipped my mind.

> *(She holds out the wrapped book.)*

NICK. Oh, it's heavy. For Brian? Really?

> *(**NICK** takes it.)*

OLIVE. I just don't know how long you'll be here and I hate having tension, any kind of tension at all, so I thought maybe this could be an olive branch of sorts. And it's important to me that he opens it himself, so the gesture is pure. That sounds so sappy. Just don't be sneaky and peek for yourself. Promise?

NICK. I'll put it right here on the table for him. That's very sweet of you.

OLIVE. Have a great day.

> *(She leaves. **NICK** closes the door. **BRIAN** peeks his head back into the room.)*

BRIAN. She's a total psycho.

NICK. I thought you went to take a shower?

BRIAN. "Oh, oh my, you've just been so nice since you [moved in…"]

NICK. [Well, I have] been nice to her. Why do you have to be so hateful?

BRIAN. I'm not.

NICK. She's been a big help to my mom. She goes to the store, brings up the mail, fucking makes her tea. You're just not used to having neighbors who give a shit.

BRIAN. How am I the [bad one here?]

NICK. [And you like not] having neighbors. Because then no one ever says, "Hey, Brian, why are you such a complete bitch to your boyfriend all the time?"

BRIAN. How's that coffee coming?

NICK. Go fuck yourself.

> *(Pause.* **NICK** *fixes a cup of coffee for himself and sits down and sips it.* **BRIAN** *watches him, waiting for more.* **NICK** *is pointedly disengaged.)*

BRIAN. I'm doing my best.

NICK. No, you're not. And you're being very dramatic.

BRIAN. Maybe…maybe I was overreacting. A little bit.

> *(***BRIAN** *steps up behind* **NICK** *and wraps his arms around him.)*

NICK. Huh.

BRIAN. Okay, I really didn't mean to bring up moving again.

NICK. Sure.

BRIAN. And the bear thing was just one of those, it was just a fluke, right?

NICK. I did put the trash out early.

BRIAN. I'm trying to apologize [to you, okay?]

NICK. [I know, but] you're just not very good at it.

> (**NICK** *steps away from* **BRIAN** *and crosses to the other side of the room.*)

BRIAN. Whoa.

NICK. Stay over there, thank you. Look, Brian, obviously I don't want you to be unhappy. I'd be sad if you left, but this is the reality of [our situation.]

BRIAN. [I'm not going] anywhere, who's saying anything about me leaving?

NICK. You just did. It happened literally minutes ago. And you bring it up a lot.

BRIAN. No, I was just talking.

NICK. We've always been good at fighting. So it's fine and all, but I'm not going to keep having the same fight. Maybe some couples do that, but it sounds sad.

BRIAN. I don't do it on purpose. And I'm…here.

NICK. I guess… I think you should take some time to think about it. About whether this is where you really want to be. Because I don't like how this feels between us; it shouldn't feel like you're doing me a favor by being here.

> (*Pause.*)

BRIAN. Fine.

NICK. Good. Oh, Olive left that for you, she's trying to build a bridge or something.

BRIAN. What is it?

NICK. Am I psychic? Open it.

BRIAN. I'll open it later. That's weird. Why's she giving me things?

NICK. You certainly don't deserve anything.

BRIAN. Oh my God, I really heard you. Don't start again.

NICK. And listen, if you want a gun, get a gun.

BRIAN. Okay.

NICK. But please don't keep it in the car. That's really fucking idiotic.

(**NICK** *heads into the back of the apartment.*)

BRIAN. Fuck.

Four

(Pamela's kitchen. The small cacti are now arranged in a "pleasing formation" on the table.)

*(**PAMELA** is quietly humming the same tune to herself while slicing vegetables on the counter. She has more scotch. The doorbell rings. She ignores it. There is a knock. She exhales, shaking her head.)*

*(**HEATHER** enters with purpose. She's wearing a similar variation of dress and cardigan from the last time she dropped by. Not the same, but she clearly has a look. She is carrying a small package wrapped in butcher paper and twine identical to the one **OLIVE** bought.)*

*(She waits, anxious and keyed-up, just inside the room as **PAMELA** continues chopping vegetables. **PAMELA**'s decidedly less chipper and clearly knows **HEATHER** is there. Waiting. Nothing but the rhythmic chopping of the knife. Finally **HEATHER**'s frustration wins out...)*

HEATHER. I used my key.

*(**PAMELA** doesn't stop. And does not look at **HEATHER**.)*

PAMELA. Maybe you should leave that key on the table.

HEATHER. Huh. If you like.

*(**HEATHER** tosses the key down on the table or the counter. Not gently.)*

I shouldn't have used it. Again. So you're right, I suppose. It's best to leave it here. Giving in to temptation can be such [a slippery...]

PAMELA. [What are you] doing here, Heather? Let's get to it. As you can see I'm very busy and I'm always going to be busy when you drop by from now until forever.

HEATHER. That's what you want to say to me?

PAMELA. I don't know what you want me to say.

HEATHER. Honey, there's no right way to [handle any of this.]

PAMELA. [But let's do agree] right now that you'll never call me "honey" again.

HEATHER. It's just a thing I say.

PAMELA. Well say something else.

HEATHER. Okay, then I'll say something else.

(**PAMELA** *stops chopping, sets down the knife, takes a drink of her scotch, and then leans forward against the counter.*)

I wanted to tell you, I wanted to say that I uprooted that butterfly bush, dug up Mr. Bundles, and I saw what you did to him, the extent of what you did to that helpless animal, and I guess I didn't know you were capable of that.

PAMELA. Oh God, you're being so fucking dramatic. This is so like you. It wasn't even your dog. You gave that dog to Jimmy. It was your husband's dog. And I know you hated having to put drops in his eyes every day.

HEATHER. Don't do me any favors, [Pamela.]

PAMELA. [Honestly, all] this over Jimmy's dog? And like [I said, I'm...]

HEATHER. [Wait. Wait,] you killed Mr. Bundles because he was Jimmy's dog?

PAMELA. I killed Mr. Bundles because even though he was a dog he acted like he was better than everything and because you gave him the most impossibly inane name in the history of pets, but mostly because I was wronged.

HEATHER. Pamela, have you completely gone insane?

PAMELA. Sometimes when someone hurts you, you have to put that hurt somewhere else.

HEATHER. Is that what you tell yourself while you drunkenly arrange your little cacti?

PAMELA. Yes.

HEATHER. I'd like for you to look at me.

>   (**PAMELA** *turns around, folds her arms, and keeps her gaze down.*)

Pamela, I'd like for you to look at me.

>   (**PAMELA** *looks up at her. Suddenly* **HEATHER** *screams...*)

It's still me!!

>   (*Pause.*)

PAMELA. I don't know what's wrong with me, Heather, I don't know what's wrong with me and I wish I could tell you that I knew what I was doing when I hurt your dog, but I just don't know, this thing, this choking thing inside me, it wasn't something I planned, I was outside with my gardening sheers and [it just...]

HEATHER. [Please stop,] the last thing I want is any kind of detail.

PAMELA. I'm trying to say I'm not proud. If you can't tell, I'm not proud.

HEATHER. But are you sorry?

PAMELA. That's not fair.

HEATHER. Pamela.

PAMELA. That's not a fair question. What about you? Are you sorry for causing me to do something that you feel I should be sorry for?

HEATHER. The vacuum cleaner sound was better than this.

PAMELA. Would you like me to get the vacuum cleaner?

HEATHER. Jesus Christ.

PAMELA. "I'm sorry," if that's what you need to hear, okay?

HEATHER. I don't "need" to hear it. I don't need you to say a damn thing. I want you to feel remorse for overreacting and doing so in such a horrific way.

PAMELA. Perhaps you should take the degree of my "overreaction" as an indicator of how very convincing you were when you made me fall in love [with you.]

HEATHER. [I know] that I [should have...]

PAMELA. [Perhaps it's] an indication of how invested I was in your stories about our future together. Perhaps there's some culpability there? And ultimately, Heather, perhaps if you are experiencing pain from the loss of your husband's dog, you could multiply that a dozen times over and know how it feels for me to stand alone in my kitchen and chop vegetables for a soup my husband will sit across from me and eat while I die inside thinking about being trapped here without all the promises your skin made because your mouth took them away. Is that possible do you think?

(Pause.)

HEATHER. I was... I was wrong to make those promises.

PAMELA. What?

HEATHER. I was wrong.

PAMELA. Ugh. Too late now. What is that you're holding?

HEATHER. It's nothing.

PAMELA. Is it a secret?

HEATHER. Stop it.

PAMELA. Your secrets end up hurting me so [let's just…]

HEATHER. [Good grief, Pamela,] I do not want to feel the way I'm feeling about you. I do not want all of the good things we shared and could still share to be poisoned.

(*She sits down at the table.*)

PAMELA. Could…still share?

HEATHER. Not like that.

PAMELA. Why not?

HEATHER. I already explained why not! Do you think that your murdering our dog changes any of that? I honestly do not understand how you can move so effortlessly between wanting to hurt me and wanting to be with me?

(**PAMELA** *sits down across from* **HEATHER.**)

PAMELA. That's a fair question.

HEATHER. It is a real question. How?

PAMELA. It's all tangled up inside me, I don't know.

HEATHER. Well, can you try a bit harder to explain? Because that answer gives me zero insight into all of this, I have no idea what to expect from you, it makes me nervous, it scares me, and I absolutely do not want things to escalate.

PAMELA. Then just tell me what the fuck you do want, Heather, because I doubt it's the same thing I want.

And I don't know what exactly you've convinced yourself since the last two times you barged into my home, but I'm very busy and this fucking soup won't make itself.

HEATHER. I want to still be able to look at you!

PAMELA. I'm just...so angry.

HEATHER. I know. But I just really wish you could show some small spark of regret for killing our dog, for that really insanely cruel and uncalled-for act, so that we have some tiny common ground. Because in spite of everything, oh God, this is the last thing I should say, Pamela, but I do love you, in a way, in a strange and confusing way. And even though I need to do what's right for me and end things, those feelings don't just go away. And I know you love me so much it's overwhelming. So I'm asking you to please not let those feelings turn into something just as intense but much less generous.

(*Pause.*)

PAMELA. Okay. Generous. Generosity isn't exactly... You're better at being generous. It's never really been my strong suit.

HEATHER. Can you at least try?

(**PAMELA** *doesn't answer.* **HEATHER** *slowly gets up from the table and begins to leave. She still has the wrapped package in hand.*)

PAMELA. You want me to be the bigger person.

HEATHER. I want us to be bigger people.

PAMELA. I'm... Okay, I never meant to... Okay, I am genuinely sorry about what I... I'm sorry that I killed Mr. Bundles.

(**HEATHER** *turns. She looks like she might cry.*)

HEATHER. Oh, Pamela, do you mean it? Really?

PAMELA. I do.

HEATHER. You have no idea what that means to me.

PAMELA. I suppose that's...good. No, it's good.

HEATHER. Yes. It's good.

PAMELA. I'm glad.

HEATHER. And I forgive you.

PAMELA. What?

HEATHER. Thank you.

> (**PAMELA** *gets up and steps away from the
> table like it might be dangerous, like it might
> be made of knives.*)

PAMELA. You forgive me?

HEATHER. Yes.

PAMELA. You fucking forgive me?

HEATHER. Why are you getting [upset?]

PAMELA. [You know, I] was actually sorry for a fraction
of a moment. Those weren't just words, okay? But then
you have to go and display, yet again, that you have all
the power in this whatever it is and I'm just here to
receive scraps from the table, unassailable edicts, and a
salt mine's worth [of hubris.]

HEATHER. [That's not what] I was doing; I'm not doing
[any of that.]

PAMELA. [You decide. You] decide. Like some fucking all-
[powerful being.]

HEATHER. [Ugh, I'm not] deciding [anything for you.]

PAMELA. [I understand.] You want forgiveness? How
about this? Tonight after Mike finishes eating this
soup, I'll bring a warm bowl over for Jimmy.

HEATHER. I don't think that [sounds like...]

PAMELA. [But isn't that] nice? And neighborly? And contrite? So contrite in fact that I'll just have to profusely apologize for having the wrong idea about sleeping with his wife.

(**HEATHER** *is clearly getting anxious. None of this sounds good.*)

HEATHER. Don't be ridiculous.

PAMELA. "I'm so sorry, Jimmy. I completely misunderstood Heather's intentions when she came over and over again at the touch of my fingers, her body shuddering, and said that she loved me. I misread the situation and that's my fault. I'm very, very sorry."

HEATHER. You know he'll tell Mike.

PAMELA. Huh. Great, ya know? Let's blow up the whole damn thing. Because maybe Mike needs to learn forgiveness, too. You can see how everyone does with your moral imperative du jour.

HEATHER. You will not do that.

PAMELA. I may very well do that so you should plan your evening accordingly.

(*Pause.*)

HEATHER. Honestly, I needed to see you like this.

PAMELA. So you can justify your sanctimonious bullshit.

HEATHER. But before I go, this is for you. I drove into Portland today and bought it in a curiosity shop as a kind of "mending fences" gift, but you can absolutely still have it because I'm just so punishingly generous, aren't I?

(**HEATHER** *sets the package on the table and steps back towards the door.*)

PAMELA. I don't want anything from you.

HEATHER. I think we both know that's not true. And you'll like this. The very attractive woman at the store helped me pick it out. She may have been flirting, but you know I'm quite devoted to my husband.

PAMELA. As of late.

HEATHER. That said, I told her about you and she knew just what to show me.

PAMELA. What is it?

HEATHER. Well it's from a curiosity shop, Pamela. So... it's a curiosity.

PAMELA. You can't bribe me into accepting [your idea of...]

HEATHER. [Oh my God, a] new Lexus with a giant bow in your driveway is a bribe; this is a gesture wrapped in butcher paper and twine.

(**PAMELA** *picks up the package.*)

PAMELA. Well whatever it is, it's heavy.

HEATHER. I'm sure you can manage.

(**PAMELA** *carries it over to the counter. She downs her scotch in one gulp and then picks up the knife she was using to chop vegetables and slices through the twine. She gives* **HEATHER** *a withering look.*)

PAMELA. But I don't have anything for you.

HEATHER. Just open it.

PAMELA. Fine.

(*Knife still in hand,* **PAMELA** *unwraps the black book. She gives* **HEATHER** *a quizzical look.* **HEATHER** *is biting her lip in anticipation.*)

(**PAMELA** *opens the front cover and pulls her hand away in pain. She looks at her hand and it is bleeding. A lot. A deafening screech of metal fills the space. The lights flicker and* **HEATHER** *has to lean against the counter or a chair for support as the stage shakes. Everything is plunged into darkness as* **PAMELA** *screams.*)

HEATHER. Pamela?? Pamela?!

(*When the lights restore it is quiet.* **PAMELA** *is gone. There is a small pile of black ash where she stood.* **HEATHER** *covers her mouth in shock.*)

Five

*(The living room again. **OLIVE** has a broom
in one hand and is emptying a dustpan of
black ash into a small trashcan.)*

*(**NICK** enters and stops at the sight of **OLIVE**.)*

OLIVE. Oh, I was just trying to straighten up a bit before
you got home. Brian left a bit of a mess and it didn't
seem like you should have to deal with [that today.]

NICK. [Left a mess,] where is Brian?

OLIVE. I'm not sure.

NICK. Olive, what is going on?

OLIVE. It's not my place to, I'm sure he'll call you.
I thought he would have called you. Whenever he,
oh, whenever he and the nice young man he was
with get back to Portland, he'll call. He said he was
going back [to Portland.]

NICK. [What nice young] man?

OLIVE. Nick, I want you to know how much I value our
friendship.

NICK. What?

OLIVE. I care about you a lot and there's that whole "don't
kill the [messenger" thing.]

NICK. [What the fuck] are you talking about?

OLIVE. Nick!

NICK. I'm sorry, I'm just a little bit confused. He hasn't
been answering my calls today. I thought it was because
I told him to take some time and think. That son of a
bitch.

OLIVE. Oh.

NICK. I can't believe it.

OLIVE. I'm guessing, I suppose you didn't know he was leaving.

NICK. No. I mean, I never thought he would.

OLIVE. He didn't have very much with him.

NICK. He didn't really ever want to come.

OLIVE. Oh, I know. You've talked about it a lot.

NICK. Huh, I guess I have.

OLIVE. Over grape leaves and hummus at Soup and Sides.

NICK. This is so surreal.

OLIVE. I'm sorry.

NICK. He left.

OLIVE. I'm so sorry.

NICK. No. You know what? No. Don't be sorry. I told him to choose and I'm glad he finally made a choice instead of just sitting around being unhappy. It's better for both of us. It's better. This is good.

OLIVE. Oh, good.

(Pause.)

NICK. God dammit.

OLIVE. You know... I was married once. I know you weren't married, but just indulge me for a minute, okay?

NICK. I never knew you were married.

OLIVE. Well, I usually don't talk about it.

NICK. As much as we've talked about my relationship, I can't believe it's never come up though. Wow.

OLIVE. Huh, listen to you. I didn't survive the wreck of the *Titanic*. It was just a marriage.

NICK. Did he leave?

OLIVE. He died.

NICK. Oh.

OLIVE. He left and then he died.

NICK. Oh.

OLIVE. Look at your face.

NICK. It's just startling. A little. To find that out.

OLIVE. It's not like I killed him.

NICK. That's not what I was [thinking.]

OLIVE. [It's okay if you] were, but I didn't kill him. He was found in bed with his new girlfriend. They burned to death in some kind of freak fire. It started with a candle, some fancy candle. Sandalwood and vanilla.

NICK. They could tell what kind of candle it was?

OLIVE. Yes? Yes. Listen, I'm not telling you this because we're having some kind of terrible news contest or to make you feel better exactly. I'm telling you this because before he left me, he had already left me. You know?

We had a lovely home in Lake Oswego. We were lucky it came on the market, the owners just up and abandoned it. They disappeared, all very mysterious. But it was my dream house, with these lovely bay windows, and because of the silly stories about what may or may not have happened in the house, we were able to get it for a steal. Anyway, I thought things were perfect. I tend to look on the bright side. But apparently, he was seeing a young woman behind my back for a while before finally getting up the courage to tell me.

And then everything was ruined. And I had to leave.

He and that girl stayed in the Lake Oswego house, my dream house. And I moved here, away from the city, away from anything to do with him.

I shouldn't say this, but between us? I'm afraid the candle that started the fire may have been one I bought him at this little shop in Portland. It was meant to bury the hatchet, let bygones be bygones. But it may very well have claimed his life along with hers and consumed that perfect home.

Wouldn't that be terrible?

But the point though, Nick, is that it was good that he left when he did because he had already moved on. And I feel like maybe we have that in common. So I suppose I'm commiserating.

(She sits next to him and puts her hand on his shoulder.)

Because of our similar situations.

NICK. That's a heartbreaking story, weird and heartbreaking. But I don't think this is like that exactly.

OLIVE. Of course it is.

NICK. I just... I don't think so.

OLIVE. No, but I [thought that...]

NICK. [Our problems] were all about moving here. Or at least moving here threw a pretty harsh light on our problems.

OLIVE. But I mean, Brian had so many other men coming and going at all hours, I just assumed that he finally [went too far.]

NICK. [How is that, how] is that any of your business?

OLIVE. I'm right downstairs, how could it not be? I could hear everything, and I mean every little thing that they did, he cheated on you; he treated [you poorly.]

NICK. [I'm no] angel, Olive. I'm not perfect. We met at a really ill-advised underwear party and did a lot of really ill-advised things. And there have been a lot of parties since then. And poor decisions, and selfish decisions, and indiscretions for both of us, I'm sure. And that's just how it is. We don't have any illusions about, well maybe I did, but we shouldn't have had any illusions about things. We were in love and that's messy but it's what matters.

OLIVE. And you think that's aspirational?

NICK. Oh God, I don't know. Who the fuck thinks about their life in that way?

OLIVE. Well, you'll pardon me, but I think that's quite sad. And regardless of historical context, I don't understand how Brian leaving you now, in the here and now, is different than what happened to me?

NICK. It just is.

    (Pause.)

OLIVE. Oh, I see. You think you're somehow better than me.

NICK. No, I don't.

OLIVE. That wasn't a question, it was a realization.

NICK. I'm kind of in the middle of my own thing right now, Olive. It's difficult to kind of get my brain off this "Brian left me" track to worry about you. I hope you can understand that doesn't mean I think anything negative.

OLIVE. I think I understand completely.

NICK. That doesn't sound like you understand completely.

OLIVE. I'm sorry I didn't say it the way you hoped.

NICK. That's not [what I meant.]

OLIVE. [Because I do] understand that perhaps I was a little too biased and maybe you and Brian deserved each other.

NICK. Where is that coming from?

OLIVE. I am trying to share with you, Nick. Because I feel like we are kindred spirits. And you are throwing that in my face. You are taking an act of kindness, of pure consideration, and throwing it right back in my face.

NICK. By disagreeing with you?

OLIVE. By disrespecting my contribution to this moment.

NICK. That isn't at all what [just happened.]

OLIVE. [Callous. I see that] now, like a shining light in a dark [cupboard.]

NICK. [Okay, I'm] gonna need you to go, please.

OLIVE. You don't think I understand? I understand that apparently neither of you is capable of caring about another person. And apparently neither of you is capable of a little thing called empathy.

NICK. Olive, I asked you to leave.

OLIVE. No, you told me to leave, told me, and after all of the time I've spent listening to you lament about your mom, your tragic relationship, that's it you know, everything is tragic with you, it hangs on you, and if you ask me, that's something [that you...]

NICK. [But nobody] asked you!

> (**OLIVE** *steps away.* **NICK** *takes a deep breath and opens and closes his fists a few times, getting his temper under control.*)

I am sorry I yelled.

> (*Instead of leaving, she sits down. It's mindboggling.*)

OLIVE. Well, I should hope so.

NICK. Could you please leave, Olive? Could you please, pretty please get the fuck out of this house? Could you go downstairs, sit alone, look inside yourself, and find some shred of understanding that this is not the time or the place for you to share these particular observations? Could you recognize that what you think about something might not be relevant or accurate at all times because it's a thought and not a fact? Could you do any of that?

(**OLIVE** *seems genuinely perplexed.*)

OLIVE. Why would I?

NICK. Olive, there is something wrong with you.

OLIVE. I'm the most normal person you'll ever meet.

NICK. Fine. I'd like to try to get in touch with my boyfriend now. So thank you for your "concern" or whatever it is and have a good day.

OLIVE. I want you to know I was always on your side, Nick.

NICK. I don't have a side.

OLIVE. Everyone has a side.

NICK. And now I'm the one who thinks that's [quite sad.]

OLIVE. [Everyone] has a side.

NICK. This is what I'm talking about; please just go.

OLIVE. We don't have to fight like this, we really don't.

NICK. We're done fighting.

OLIVE. I just can't stand for things to be awkward.

NICK. You can work on that.

OLIVE. Let me make it up to you; let me take you to Soup and Sides?

NICK. No, I don't [want to go to Soup and...]

OLIVE. [I know, let's go] and visit your mom, I'm sure she'd love to see both [of us.]

NICK. [No. No, that's...]

OLIVE. How about we head [over to…?]

NICK. [No!]

>*(Pause. **OLIVE** starts to say something, but…)*

No!!!!

>*(**OLIVE** leaves. **NICK** squeezes his fists and begins to shake with rage. It passes. He shakes out his hands.)*

Okay. Okay. Okay.

Six

(A mostly bare room. Odds and ends. It might have a bit of a workshop feel. There is a single, very solid wooden chair with a small end table next to it. On the end table there is an ashtray and an exact replica of the odd dictaphone or radio-like machine on the counter in the shop. Well, this one may be more beat up.)

(A scrim behind the set illuminates for the first time to reveal a piece of an immense, deep orange circle. It is gigantic and truly dwarfs the rest of the set. Behind the orange circle is a bright yellow and white background that glows and churns. It is intense. It's Mercury in front of the Sun.)

(The lighting in the room itself is warm and dim, like a light inside of an oven. There are bright patches, ethereal. There is a low throbbing of a deep bass sound somewhere in the background. It's something large turning slowly.)

*(**PAMELA** is sitting in the only chair. She still has the small black book and the knife she was holding in her kitchen. **BRIAN**, still in his T-shirt and underwear, is lying on his back on the floor staring up into space. He also has the small black book in his hands, holding it on his chest.)*

BRIAN. It's like the inside of an oven.

(Pause.)

It feels like the inside of an oven.

(*Pause.*)

Doesn't it?

PAMELA. You keep trying to talk to me and it keeps not working. Learn.

BRIAN. I'm not good at quiet.

PAMELA. I'm not good at killing time humoring stray observations about the temperature.

BRIAN. Are you very busy with your own thoughts?

PAMELA. Yes.

(*Pause.*)

BRIAN. Maybe we're in Hell.

PAMELA. It's not Hell.

BRIAN. How would we know?

PAMELA. I think we'd be on fire.

BRIAN. It's really fucking hot.

PAMELA. And in a lot of pain.

BRIAN. Okay.

PAMELA. It has to... Ugh, it has to do with these fucking books.

BRIAN. Right?

PAMELA. Blank fucking books.

BRIAN. They're not blank.

PAMELA. What?

BRIAN. Mine's not blank. There's a little handwritten page right in the middle. I found it during the silence of your very lengthy anti-social period.

(**PAMELA** *flips through her book to the middle and stops on a page.*)

PAMELA. "When I am working on a problem, I never think about beauty but when I have finished, if the solution is not beautiful, I know it is wrong." – R. Buckminster Fuller

BRIAN. Yep. Same quote in mine.

PAMELA. Well now it's even worse.

BRIAN. And it's handwritten in purple ink. That's weird.

PAMELA. Oh, that's the weird thing?

BRIAN. He was a pretty famous architect, I think.

PAMELA. He can take his "beautiful solutions" and fuck off.

BRIAN. You're super pleasant.

PAMELA. Are you fucking kidding me?

BRIAN. Look, I'm doing my best. It's been hours.

PAMELA. It feels like days.

> *(Somewhere in the distance, people start screaming. It is blood curdling and it sounds like several people. In real pain.* **PAMELA** *winces.* **BRIAN** *covers his ears. It eventually stops.)*

> *(Pause.)*

BRIAN. So... I got the book as a gift from my downstairs neighbor. My boyfriend's downstairs neighbor. Actually, my boyfriend's mom's downstairs [neighbor.]

PAMELA. [Okay, I get] it, you're super progressive.

BRIAN. She hated me.

PAMELA. She sounds smart.

BRIAN. She did this. Whatever this is.

PAMELA. Why did she hate you?

BRIAN. I guess because I hated her. And I hated moving to the mountains, and I hated my new hospital, and I hated the stupid fucking bears.

PAMELA. Bears?

BRIAN. I basically hated everything. Oh God, did I hate everything?

PAMELA. Wait, so you did something terrible to this neighbor woman?

BRIAN. What? No. I never did anything to Olive. Not anything actually bad.

PAMELA. Olive, huh? Well, I don't think I know her, so she's not the reason I'm here.

BRIAN. Where'd you get your book?

PAMELA. I...found it.

BRIAN. Super believable.

PAMELA. Fine. My married next-door neighbor gave it to me after she told me she didn't want to fuck anymore because I suppose I fell in love.

BRIAN. Did your husband know?

PAMELA. Excuse me?

BRIAN. I mean, you're wearing a wedding ring so I figure [you have a...]

PAMELA. [Look at you] with your eyes that work.

BRIAN. Perfect. We'll just sit here forever in silence.

PAMELA. You can try to climb up the wall again. That was really successful.

BRIAN. At least I tried something.

> (*Somewhere in the distance, people start screaming again.* **PAMELA** *curls up in the chair.* **BRIAN** *covers his ears. It eventually stops.*)

PAMELA. No. My husband didn't know.

BRIAN. Are you sure?

PAMELA. And he's not creative enough to have done this.

BRIAN. Why do you have that knife?

PAMELA. I think because I was holding it when I opened the book.

BRIAN. I wish I had been wearing pants. Which is, like, not how I usually feel.

PAMELA. I wish I had been holding a bottle of scotch.

BRIAN. I change my wish. I wish for that, too.

PAMELA. Fuck, I need scotch.

(*Pause.*)

BRIAN. Someone has to come for us, right?

PAMELA. But is that a good thing?

BRIAN. We can't stay trapped in here forever.

PAMELA. Why not?

BRIAN. Oh God.

PAMELA. All the doors are sealed. No windows. It's just a whole lot of nothing, which is seriously disheartening. I don't know, maybe it is Hell.

BRIAN. I'd hate to think I deserve to be in Hell.

PAMELA. Okay, what is your name?

BRIAN. Brian.

PAMELA. Brian, I'm Pamela. And whatever this is, I definitely do not deserve it.

> (**SAM** *enters. Other than a worn, messy leather apron, he's completely naked. Maybe he's fully naked and carrying the leather*

apron to put on when he sees **PAMELA** *and* **BRIAN**. *Either way, he's also covered in blood. Not entirely. Just up to his elbows on his arms, and from his feet and legs all the way to mid way up his torso. As if he waded through a pool of blood. His hands and forearms in particular drip with blood. He's pretty casual though. Annoyed but chill.* **PAMELA** *sits still.* **BRIAN** *takes a step back.*)

(**SAM** *is carrying a handheld "brick"-style vaporizer in his free hand. When he takes drags off of it, the smoke he exhales is thick and voluminous.*)

SAM. You wanna get the fuck out of my chair?

(**PAMELA** *quickly gets up and hides behind* **BRIAN**. *But* **BRIAN** *moves so they're next to each other.*)

Great.

PAMELA. Are you going to hurt us?

SAM. Not both of you.

(**PAMELA** *and* **BRIAN** *look at each other.* **SAM** *stretches a bit.*)

PAMELA. Where are we?

SAM. That's tricky.

BRIAN. Maybe don't piss him off.

PAMELA. Shut up, I want to know where we are.

(*While he continues,* **SAM** *sits down.*)

SAM. It would be hard to explain.

PAMELA. Try me.

SAM. Have you ever stared directly into the sun for any length of time?

BRIAN. No.

PAMELA. Of course not.

SAM. Well, anyway, we're near that.

>*(He takes a deep drag off the vaporizer and exhales a cloud of smoke. He continues to do this throughout the scene. It's rote behavior.)*

PAMELA. That...that doesn't mean anything.

SAM. To you.

PAMELA. That doesn't mean anything to anyone.

SAM. We value your feedback.

BRIAN. Are you... Why are you covered in blood?

SAM. Good question. You want me to show you?

>*(**PAMELA** holds out the knife.)*

PAMELA. You have no idea what I'm capable of doing.

>*(**SAM** is suddenly up out of the chair and moving. He grabs her face with one hand by the chin. He stares into her eyes. She begins to shudder as a rumble shakes the floor.)*

>*(Sidelight cuts into the space from behind him. **SAM**'s voice is suddenly amplified as his words spill out like rushing water, as if he's watching all of what he's describing speed by and adding moments of his own commentary.)*

SAM. I bet you think you're fucking clever, think you're scary, but I already know you're capable of deception and deceit, you lie to get what you want, you've done it since you were a child, emotional blackmail, false tears and tantrums, cutting off your own hair as a little girl over the color of a balloon you didn't like, something as silly as a Mylar balloon, your poor parents, and in order to not feel guilty or responsible over time you became exceptional at justifying those lies as stepping stones to happiness even though you'll never really be happy because in your mind acquiring something only leads to wanting something new, this compulsion, tight in your chest, this feeling of deep dissatisfaction that permeates every little gesture, and you're much more about the power of accomplishing than the satisfaction of having, as evidenced by the fact you married a man you didn't love in order to have the wedding and recognition you always thought you deserved from the people around you, in an ivory empire waist wedding gown that was actually quite beautiful, good for you, even though your mother wasn't there, she was at home crying because you didn't invite her because it was the only weapon you had left to hurt her just to see if you could still inflict damage, although you framed the entire drama as proving a point about your independence, but it was all just another Mylar balloon, that said the only thing you've ever physically injured in your entire life besides yourself is a Cavalier King Charles Spaniel that you recently killed and you cried the entire time you were stabbing the animal and then the entire time you were burying it under a really lovely, deep purple butterfly bush, sobbing into the bloody dirt, but it wasn't the act that upset you, instead you just felt like you were supposed to cry over lost love and the lengths you had to go to feel vindication and validation for your broken heart, a heart that isn't really broken because it was never whole to start with and that's nobody's fault except your own.

> *(He releases her and she crumples to the floor, dropping the knife. The sound fades and the lights restore.* **SAM***'s voice also returns to normal.)*

SAM. So I mean I mostly do know what you're capable of, Pamela. And I'm not super worried about it. Okay? Oh, did you want a turn, Brian?

BRIAN. No. No, thank you.

SAM. Look, I'm trying to be polite but you have no idea what's going on and I've pretty clearly been wading through all kinds of horrors this morning so let's all just acknowledge the danger in that and acknowledge that if you were even a little bit nicer you probably wouldn't be here so maybe dial back the entitlement a tick.

> *(Somewhere in the distance, people start screaming again. **PAMELA** and **BRIAN** cover their ears. **SAM** smokes and examines them. It eventually stops.)*

Now as you can tell things here are kind of busy, so let's just get to it. Both of you have that book?

BRIAN. Yes.

SAM. Ugh, that is so fucking annoying.

> *(**SAM** grabs the books out of each of their hands, slams them down on the side table, and then sits again. He picks up the funnel of the dictaphone and speaks.)*

Could you please join me on the threshing floor?

PAMELA. The threshing floor?

> *(**SAM** hangs up the funnel.)*

SAM. There's only one copy of this book for a reason and it's so we don't end up in a situation like this where I'm having to take time out of my day to deal with multiple terrible people showing up on the same claim ticket.

PAMELA. I am not a terrible person.

SAM. Did you feel how those words got caught in your throat? And you had to force it out? That's because it was too much to swallow. You have anything to add?

BRIAN. No.

SAM. I feel like it's coming though...?

BRIAN. No.

SAM. Great.

BRIAN. It's just that you said there's only one book?

SAM. Yep.

BRIAN. But we each got a book.

SAM. No, you each got the book.

BRIAN. I don't understand.

SAM. Maybe get used to that feeling. Look...

> (*He picks up the book off the side table. It's one black book now, instead of two.*)

One book.

> (**ALICIA** *enters. She's barefoot in jeans and a tank top with her hair pulled up in a knot. She's still wearing the gloves.*)

ALICIA. Ugh, Sam, I don't know, they just won't stop screaming and I'm honestly getting kind of frustrated. Oh! Oh, I didn't know you were working.

SAM. No, this is perfect. This is why I wanted you. Let's have a chat. You know this black book, the one with the Buckminster Fuller quote?

ALICIA. Um, I'm the one who wrote it in there with my lucky pen. Oh God, that's such a great quote, right? "When I am working on a problem, I never think about beauty but when I have finished, if the solution is not beautiful, I know it is wrong." I feel like it's really just such a perfect thought. It makes that book way better.

SAM. I happen to agree.

ALICIA. Mmhm.

SAM. Mmhm, but somehow both of these people had a copy. I don't know how that could happen though because we only ever sell it to one person at a time.

(**ALICIA** *just sighs. She looks annoyed.*)

How do you think that happened?

ALICIA. I don't know, Sam, but if you're going to start off by being so patronizing then I guess we'll never get to the bottom of this really important mystery.

(*She takes off her gloves for the first time to reveal hands that are permanently stained black with soot. They look like she's been working in a coal mine for decades without a break. She shoves the gloves in her back pocket.*)

SAM. I'm trying to express my frustration.

ALICIA. Then say you're frustrated.

SAM. I am very frustrated.

ALICIA. Tone.

SAM. Alicia, I'm really fucking frustrated.

ALICIA. Okay. Well look, you know Olive? She comes in all the time. And the book was just perfect for her needs. Does one of you know Olive?

BRIAN. That's me.

ALICIA. She's so great, right? Anyway, right after she left another really pretty lady came in and someone killed her dog and broke her heart. So I [figured that...]

PAMELA. [I did not break] her heart! She broke my heart!

SAM. I'm gonna need you to not interrupt. If you do it again, I'll sew your lips shut. I don't mean that metaphorically. I will take a nail and some twine and actually sew your mouth shut, okay? I mean it's so fucking rude.

ALICIA. So I figured it'd work out that they wouldn't gift the book at the same time. I'm fully aware that "there's only one book, don't mess with reality" and all that stuff.

SAM. That "stuff" is the fabric of space and time.

ALICIA. In my defense, they both really seemed to be in need. And honestly, how was I supposed to know they'd both be so fucking eager to incinerate people alive? That's just very aggressive.

> (**SAM**'s *voice begins to amplify again and the lights begin to darken.*)

SAM. Alicia, I don't understand. I'm trying, honestly. I'm doing my best to be supportive and communicate clearly, but how many times have I told you that you can't just fucking do whatever you want?!

ALICIA. Okay, in the spirit of honesty, I'm scared, I'm expressing that I'm scared.

SAM. Good.

ALICIA. And you know I respect your whole "physical manifestation of vengeance" thing.

SAM. Good.

ALICIA. But in our last session, the therapist said that I should not allow myself to be intimidated by you when you act out. I will not relinquish my power. It is my shop. Mine. And if I'm willing to go back and forth, and you know that's not an easy trip, in order to sell your handiwork, then you need to not be mad with me right now.

(**SAM** *exhales and crashes down into the chair. The lights restore, his voice returns to normal. He takes a huge drag off of his vaporizer.*)

ALICIA. And...I'm, like, sorry. Okay?

SAM. You know I have to send one of them back now.

ALICIA. Both of those women know about the additional costs and penalties. I totally told them about the additional costs and penalties.

SAM. Fine.

ALICIA. I love you.

SAM. Then why don't you ever listen?

ALICIA. I do listen. I just do something different sometimes. And I fully think you're grumpy because Mercury is in retrograde.

(*She points to Mercury.*)

But I'll tell you about it later because I really need to finish skinning these people now or my whole day's gonna be thrown off.

BRIAN. Oh, fuck.

ALICIA. Oh no, you two ignore that part. I'll try to keep it down. But I do have to be quick, Sam, because I still need to run by the grocery store and pick up a cake for tonight.

SAM. What's tonight?

ALICIA. Dinner with Jack and Beverly.

SAM. Seriously?

ALICIA. I told them I'd make something for dessert. But there's literally no time, so if I put the store cake in Tupperware they won't even know the difference. Just be ready at six and wear a tie. Love you.

(She crosses over, kisses him on the cheek, and then exits.)

SAM. Okay. Okay, here's the thing... I can only have one ticket on this book at a time. And clearly there are two people out there who hated or feared you enough to convince Alicia that she should bend the rules. But that's not how it's gonna play out, so I'm going to have to send one of you back. But only one of you. And getting back is not a pleasant process, but it's frankly a lot better than being dead, right? So you'll be fine with it.

*(**BRIAN** and **PAMELA** both perk up considerably.)*

BRIAN. Who gets to go back?

SAM. Oh right, you'd think we'd have some kind of grand process for that, but we don't. Because this isn't supposed to fucking happen. You two will just figure it out. Amongst yourselves. Go ahead.

(He takes a long drag off the vaporizer and exhales the smoke towards them.)

Please decide faster.

BRIAN. Well, I'd like to go back.

*(**PAMELA** laughs at him.)*

What?

PAMELA. I'd also like to go back. My, my husband must be worried sick, he can't do anything without me, oh, and I just bought a bunch of cacti that need to be watered.

BRIAN. Oh come on, you don't even have to water cacti.

PAMELA. That's funny, I didn't realize you were some kind of secret expert on desert plants.

BRIAN. I don't have to be an expert to know they're a really stupid reason to go back.

(**PAMELA** *transforms entirely into someone
sincere. She sells this hard.*)

PAMELA. Brian, this is so hard. But I honestly don't think
Heather ever would have given me that book if she
knew what it was going to do, if she knew I would end
up here. She doesn't hate me and she's not afraid of me.
I'm harmless. I just got confused and made a mistake,
I'm aware of that now and I just want to go back to
my life. This was an awful misunderstanding and while
of course I feel terrible asking you to help me in this
way, asking you to be so selfless, I can promise that if
you let me go back, I'll live for the both of us and I will
absolutely treasure every single day.

BRIAN. Wait. Was all of that serious?

PAMELA. Of course.

BRIAN. No. No, I was in this room with you for a small
eternity before this guy showed up and now you're
what, just a completely different person? I'm not going
to fall for that. It sounds like you did some terrible
things to end up here.

(**PAMELA** *drops the act.*)

PAMELA. And you didn't?

BRIAN. No. Not exactly. I mean, yes. Yes, I was childish
and selfish, but [I didn't...]

PAMELA. [And now] you want to go back to the life you
told me you hated?

BRIAN. It sounds like you want the same thing.

(*She very overtly collects her knife from the
floor.*)

PAMELA. Okay. How do you want to figure it out?

BRIAN. What's with the knife?

PAMELA. It's my knife; we covered this.

BRIAN. Well we're not going to have a knife fight.

PAMELA. No, we're not. We'd need two knives for that.

BRIAN. Just listen to me for a second, all right?

PAMELA. Go ahead.

BRIAN. Good. Good. Because I think I have a plan. It doesn't do us any good to compare lives, neither of us is just going to give up. You want to go back. I definitely want to go back and at least try to be better for Nick, for myself, and stop being such an asshole all the time. So look, I think if we both refuse to choose then…

> (**PAMELA** *stabs him in the stomach.*)

PAMELA. Sorry, Brian. But if I've learned anything it's that life's not always fair.

> (*She pulls the knife out and* **BRIAN** *falls to his knees bleeding.*)

BRIAN. Holy shit.

PAMELA. Okay, we decided I'm going back.

> (**SAM** *starts clapping and crosses over to* **PAMELA**. *He gently takes the knife from her hand.*)

SAM. Pamela, maybe I was wrong about your capabilities. I'm willing to own that. So here's the thing. Like I said, getting back is a little bit of a process. There's this whole warm-to-warm, blood-to-blood thing, you don't have to understand it. But there are definitely a few things we should cover, Brian, just information you'll need. Before you go back.

PAMELA. You mean, Pamela.

SAM. Oh no, I can tell the difference between you.

PAMELA. I'm the one going back.

SAM. It's funny you keep saying that because you really showed me something just now. And what you showed me is that you seriously fucking belong here.

BRIAN. Oh wow.

PAMELA. No, I don't! I do not belong here.

SAM. I mean that regardless of whoever you were, a very strong case can be made for the fact that you belong here now. Which means Brian was wronged more by being sent here and has a better case for seeking revenge. And I'm supposed to care about those kinds of things, confidentially. Also, and don't take this the wrong way, he just generally seems, between the two of you, like a better person.

PAMELA. What?!

> (**BRIAN** *quietly begins to laugh. Coughing, bleeding from a knife wound, and laughing. And* **PAMELA** *visibly begins to panic.*)

SAM. Oh sure, there's no way you're going back. You're a fucking menace. You earned your spot here in just the most exquisite way, just [so obvious.]

PAMELA. [You said for us] to figure it out and we did!

SAM. Oh no, I saw that. It happened right in [front of me.]

PAMELA. [This is bullshit!] And what? I don't get any justice?! Heather just gets to live her life, just gets to carry on like nothing ever happened, like I don't even matter.

SAM. I mean...she'll probably feel bad.

> (**BRIAN** *starts laughing maniacally.*)

PAMELA. This is not fair! It's not fair!

SAM. Well as much as it pains me to quote you back to yourself, life's not always fair. And since you brought her up...

> (**HEATHER** *enters. Her hair is perfect. Her makeup is perfect. She's wearing a variation of her familiar outfit, but in all black. She's carrying a hacksaw in one hand and has a shovel over her other shoulder.*)

> (**BRIAN** *stops laughing and pushes himself along the floor away from her, clearly scared and worried about his own safety.*)

PAMELA. Oh my God.

SAM. You really do have to be careful about manifesting things around me, Pamela. I'm always looking for just the right solution to a problem. And, of course, hoping it will be beautiful.

PAMELA. What are you doing here? What is Heather doing here?

SAM. Now don't be dense. Heather's in her lovely home outside of Portland with her husband drinking a crisp California Shiraz and looking through breeder books for a new dog. Honestly, you'd just hate it.

PAMELA. But this is Heather, I think [I know Heather.]

> (**HEATHER** *presents with an excited smile and terrifying eyes.*)

HEATHER. [Oh, I just love] you so much, Pamela, let's be together forever, it's just so overwhelming, you know, I can't contain all of this passion, I just want to cut you up into little pieces and bury you under a gorgeous butterfly bush so I know where you are forever, so you're with me forever.

PAMELA. What the fuck?

HEATHER. I'm going to use this hacksaw to cut you up into pieces and bury you under a gorgeous butterfly bush; I'm going to kiss each little piece as it goes into the dirt.

PAMELA. No, please, no.

HEATHER. Yes!

PAMELA. Please don't do this to me.

SAM. Don't look at me. You did this.

PAMELA. I'm sorry, really, [I'm so sorry.]

HEATHER. [Oh my God, you're so] beautiful when you apologize I can barely contain how much I love you and want to lovingly saw through your flesh and bone then put you in the ground piece by piece every day [over and over again.]

PAMELA. [No, no, no, no...]

> (**PAMELA** *tries to run.* **SAM** *grabs her wrist. She is freaking out, but his hold on her looks effortless. He drags her offstage but casually looks over at* **BRIAN**...)

SAM. Great. Now tell me, Brian, are there any itinerant people or large wild animals where you live?

> (**BRIAN** *follows* **SAM** *and* **PAMELA** *off.* **HEATHER** *skips after them with a smile.)*

Seven

(The living room again. **ALICIA** *is wearing a winter coat now, gloves back on, and has the enormous knife from earlier in a sheath strapped around her thigh. She's examining a large dead bear carcass in the center of the floor. Maybe there's a trail of blood leading to it.)*

(Her cell phone rings with a cute sound. She fishes it out of her coat pocket.)

ALICIA. Are you fucking kidding me?

(She answers it.)

Hey. Yes. Yes. Well you didn't say he lived on the second floor. Do you have any idea how fucking heavy a dead bear is in reality?

Only like twenty minutes ago, it's still warm. It'll work, okay.

It took so long because shockingly there's no rope and pulley system handy so I had to drag it up a flight of stairs and it's a really enormous bear. I'm moving big machinery, I'm dragging dead animals around, I'm running the shop, so don't you get pissed with me, Sam.

Yes you are. We've been dating for one hundred and twenty-seven years, I can tell when you're pissed off.

I always bring it up because I don't see a ring on my finger.

That's right you're sorry. Look, I killed it myself so I know it's fresh and it's right where you said to put it. So you're all set. Can I get out of here now?

Ugh, do I really have to do that?

Fine. Whatever. Love you. Bye.

(She hangs up the phone. She pulls out her knife and cuts a huge gash down the middle of the bear's stomach. Blood runs out. Satisfied, she leaves.)

(After a moment, the lights shift to darker hues, shadows creeping in and moving, as a soft glow rises on the bear's carcass. The light shift is accompanied by a very loud and harsh screeching of metal on metal. The carcass begins to writhe from the inside. A hand breaks free of the body through the gash Alicia cut, then another hand. **BRIAN** *slowly drags himself from inside the bear back into the living world. He is a mess, still in the same clothes but now covered in blood from his horrific journey through the animal. And of course he's still bloody from being stabbed by Pamela earlier.)*

(He pulls himself away from the bear and tries to get up as blood spills from his mouth. But he's laughing. Smiling. He's happy to be back in this apartment, familiar surroundings. Once he's free of the bear, the lights return and the sounds dissipate. He calls out, but he's still coughing up blood.)

BRIAN. Nick? Nick, are you here? Nick?!

(But Nick isn't home. Something occurs to **BRIAN.** *He looks down at the floor then kneels down placing an ear to it. He smiles, gets up, heads over to the door, moves just to the side of it and begins to scream. It is an awful, full-throated scream of terror. He stops and waits.)*

*(***OLIVE** *can be heard before she bursts into the room.)*

OLIVE. Nick?! Oh my God, are you okay?! I heard the shouting and I...

> *(She stops at the sight of the bear carcass. Behind her, **BRIAN** steps out and blocks the door. Effectively trapping **OLIVE** in the apartment.)*

Oh heavens.

BRIAN. Hello, Olive.

OLIVE. Oh God! Oh my God, [Brian. Oh my God.]

BRIAN. [Just look at this] crazy mess. I hope none of it bleeds down into your place, but if it does, I will absolutely pick up the cleaning bill.

OLIVE. Oh my God.

BRIAN. Or maybe we'll just split it.

OLIVE. I thought you were, I [thought you...]

BRIAN. [Uh huh?]

OLIVE. How are you here?

BRIAN. How am I here?

OLIVE. I mean, I meant where have you been? Nick has been beside himself with [worry.]

BRIAN. [Stop.]

OLIVE. We had no idea where you'd gone? Nick thought you ran off [with some...]

BRIAN. [I said] stop. And don't casually say "we" when you talk about yourself and my boyfriend in the same sentence. And don't act like I'm not standing here next to a fucking dead bear covered in blood. I know what you did, Olive.

OLIVE. Are you bleeding?

BRIAN. A woman named Pamela stabbed me. I think you'd really like her.

OLIVE. Should we call a doctor?

BRIAN. I am a fucking doctor.

OLIVE. You're a physician's assistant.

BRIAN. I want to know why you gave me that book?!

OLIVE. What book? Oh, the journal? It was, it was a peace offering.

BRIAN. Fuck you.

OLIVE. Maybe if you were nicer to [people then...]

BRIAN. [I want you] to be really careful about how you finish that sentence because I've already been down that [road today.]

OLIVE. [You see that?] You're impossible, I just can't talk to you at all. And the way you treat Nick, disrespect Nick, it's simply unconscionable.

BRIAN. I'm astonished, I am really [fucking astonished.]

OLIVE. [I was trying] to fix a problem. When I see a problem, I make it right. I'm not afraid to make [it right.]

BRIAN. [So you killed] me?!

OLIVE. No! I absolutely did nothing of the sort. You're standing right there, alive, breathing, and you sound insane, just [completely insane.]

BRIAN. [I'm not buying] it, Olive. No one is buying it.

OLIVE. Whatever kind of delusional breakdown you're experiencing in here, with the blood and the screaming, it has nothing to do with me! Maybe you should take a hard look in the mirror, at your choices, at your own relationship, [and try to...]

BRIAN. [Holy fuck, how] could you know anything about my relationship at all, from the outside, and why is it any of your business? The questions are [innumerable.]

OLIVE. [Brian, honestly,] whatever this is that's happening to you, if it's happening because of that little book then I deeply regret reaching out with a gift. I obviously had no idea what [would happen.]

BRIAN. [Then why the] fuck did you give it to me, Olive?!

OLIVE. I told you why.

BRIAN. Because you care.

OLIVE. Yes.

BRIAN. About Nick.

OLIVE. Yes.

BRIAN. And about Nick's mom, too?

(*Pause.*)

OLIVE. I am sure I don't know what you're talking about.

BRIAN. I'm sure you do with all your visits and all of your concern.

OLIVE. I'm not capable of whatever you're implying.

BRIAN. Then how do you know what I'm implying?

OLIVE. I would never [do anything to…]

BRIAN. [Made a few] trips to that shop before, huh?

OLIVE. How do you know about the shop?

BRIAN. Really?! Look at me, [really?!]

OLIVE. [You're] getting very angry [and I…]

BRIAN. [Yep!]

OLIVE. And I can see that you've already been quite violent.

BRIAN. Me?! I've been violent?

OLIVE. Just look at this poor animal! I truly believe you're having a psychotic episode of [some kind.]

BRIAN. [I didn't kill that] bear, Olive. If I had killed that bear, I would have done it with a shotgun but you already know that from always listening, listening and plotting.

OLIVE. I do not plot and I will not stand [here and...]

BRIAN. [You gave me a] book that incinerated me and sent me to Hell! And if it wasn't Hell it was at least someplace I never want to be again.

OLIVE. Who in the world would ever believe that story?

BRIAN. You will after you pay it a visit! And I'm fucking thrilled to facilitate that trip!

(She begins to back away from him.)

OLIVE. Oh God, please don't hurt me.

BRIAN. I'm not going to hurt you. I should hurt you for me and for Nick and for Nick's mom. Just tell me what you're doing to Nick's mom. I can at least do that much for him.

OLIVE. I told you I'm not [doing anything.]

(He explodes towards her, menacing.)

BRIAN. [Tell me or I'll completely] lose my shit!!

OLIVE. It's the tea bags! I got the tea bags from that shop! If she stops drinking the chamomile I bring her then I guess she'll get better.

BRIAN. You guess?

OLIVE. I don't ask a lot of questions.

BRIAN. So you do go to that shop and you are doing all of [this on purpose.]

OLIVE. [I promise I'll] stop, Brian. This has been, this has been very eye opening; this is one of those moments that totally changes a person's perspective on things. And I just, I feel like I should go back downstairs and really [think about...]

BRIAN. [Please shut the] fuck up!

OLIVE. You said you're not going to hurt me and I want to go.

BRIAN. Admit what you did first. Say it!

OLIVE. Please let me go.

BRIAN. I wish it were that easy, Olive. But you've messed with other people's lives and there's a little thing called karma that we should really talk about [before you go.]

OLIVE. [I don't, I don't] believe in karma. This is ridiculous and I will not abide it. I know you know deep down inside somewhere that you got exactly what you deserved.

BRIAN. No, I don't!

OLIVE. Somewhere way down [deep in your...]

BRIAN. [Fucking dig me] apart, Olive, you will never find a piece of me that feels like I deserve you and your sense of righteous whatever [the fuck.]

OLIVE. [You will not] lay blame at my feet. You reap what you sow.

BRIAN. Well, you just described karma in a nutshell, which apparently you don't believe in, so maybe go do your fucking homework!

OLIVE. You think you're so smart? Fine. But I know the difference between right and wrong! You might not agree with my methods and maybe they were not the most societally acceptable for whatever that's worth, but that woman lived here for years and thoughtlessly infringed on my personal space without any hesitation and then you show up and are honestly one of the most selfish, dishonest, malcontent human beings I've ever encountered. Ever! And that's saying a lot! I will not be maligned, I will not be made to feel small, and for the love of God, I only gave you a stupid book!

BRIAN. To teach me a lesson!

OLIVE. Yes!

BRIAN. Because I deserved to die!

OLIVE. Yes, okay! Yes! I wanted you to die!

> *(The lights shift back to the darker hues with a glow on the bear's carcass and the screeching of metal.* **BRIAN** *relaxes.* **OLIVE** *notices the shifting environment.)*

BRIAN. Thank you for finally saying it.

OLIVE. What's happening?

BRIAN. I'm not sure exactly. I did my part. But apparently there was some chitchat about the potential for additional costs and penalties?

OLIVE. Not really?

BRIAN. Are you sure someone named Alicia didn't tell you about the additional costs and penalties involved in damning someone for eternity?

OLIVE. I don't know.

BRIAN. That's a real fucking shame because a guy named Sam told me that there definitely are some, Olive. I mean, I heard the people screaming.

OLIVE. Well, I'm sure Alicia will explain [everything to me...]

BRIAN. [I really don't think] she will.

OLIVE. Why not?

BRIAN. Goodbye, Olive.

*(Suddenly, **SAM** erupts out of the bear's carcass, dragging himself into the world and exhaling a plume of smoke as he emerges. He is still in the apron but otherwise naked and mostly covered in blood. He grapples **OLIVE** as she protests in horror. He's very much all business as **OLIVE** struggles and screams for help. She reaches towards **BRIAN**, but he stumbles back away from her.)*

OLIVE. Oh God! Oh my God, no! Let go of [me! Help! Get off me! Brian, don't let him take me! Please! Someone help me!]

SAM. [Come on, now. Let's not make this difficult. I've got other things to do today.]

*(She continues to scream as **SAM** picks her up and carries her out of the apartment. It's almost as if they vanish into the sounds and darkness. The lights return to normal and everything goes quiet.)*

BRIAN. Holy shit.

*(**BRIAN** collapses onto the ground. He gets his hair out of his face and then tries to wipe some of the blood off his hands and arms, but it's basically everywhere.)*

*(**NICK** enters carrying cardboard boxes. He immediately drops them when he sees **BRIAN** and the bear carcass.)*

NICK. Whoa! Whoa.

BRIAN. It's okay.

NICK. It is not okay. Brian, what are you doing here? Why is there a dead bear in the living room? Answer the second part first.

BRIAN. I'm sorry.

NICK. You're sorry?

BRIAN. Yes, I'm sorry. For just, for everything.

NICK. That's not an answer. That doesn't explain this dead animal horror show in the living room or why you're covered in blood.

BRIAN. It's mostly not my blood.

NICK. Oh God, Brian, that's not better. Where have you been? You've been gone for weeks [and now you just…]

BRIAN. [Wait, how long] have I been gone?

NICK. Fucking weeks. Why don't you [know that?]

BRIAN. [It was really] hard to [tell exactly.]

NICK. [Oh my God, are] you bleeding? What the fuck is going on?

> (**BRIAN** *kisses* **NICK**. *The moment settles.*)

BRIAN. You're here, so I'm here. Nick, I want to…

> (*He sits down. The knife wound in his stomach becoming more insistent now that his Olive "mission" has concluded.* **NICK** *helps him.*)

NICK. It's okay, sit down.

BRIAN. I'll try to explain it all to you, about Olive and the book and the shop and your mom and that bear, but just… I'm not going anywhere. You're here so I'm here. I'm here.

> (**BRIAN** *smiles. He's sure. Lights crash to black.*)

End of Play